Goodnight, Goodnight, Construction Site

Goodnight, Goodnight, Construction Site

SHERRI DUSKEY RINKER AND TOM LICHTENHELD

SCHOLASTIC INC.
New York Toronto London Auckland
Sydney Mexico City New Delhi Hong Kong

Down in the big construction site,
The tough trucks work with all their might
To build a building, make a road,
To get the job done—load by load!

The sun has set, the work is done;
It's time for trucks to end their fun.
So one by one they'll go to bed
To yawn and rest their sleepy heads,
Then wake up to another day
Of rough-and-tough construction play!

Working hard to help his team,
Crane Truck raises one last beam.

Reaching, stretching, lifting high,
He swings the beam into the sky.
He'll set it down right on its mark,
Then off to bed; it's almost dark.

He slowly folds his boom back in,
And then with one last sleepy grin,
He tucks himself in nice and tight (*sigh!*),
Then cuddles up and says goodnight.

Shh . . . goodnight, Crane Truck, goodnight.

Spinning, churning all day long,
Cement Mixer sings his whirly song.

Now (*yawn!*) he's weary

and so dizzy,

From the fun that keeps him busy.

With one last spin, he pours the load.
He's ready now to leave the road.

He takes a bath, gets shiny-bright,
Pulls up his chute, turns off his light.

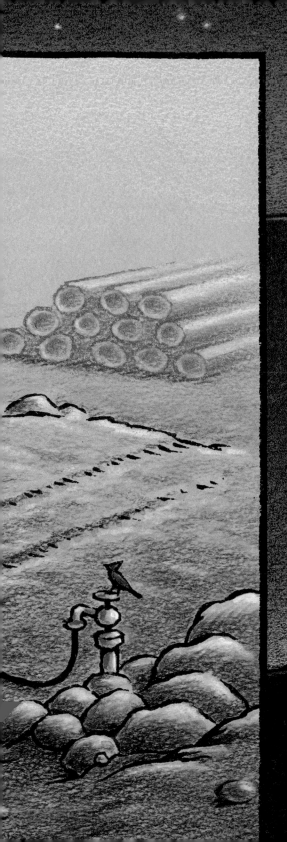

He cuts his engine, slows his drum,
And dreams sweet dreams of twirly fun.

Shh . . . goodnight, Cement Mixer, goodnight.

Dump Truck loves to work and haul.   He carries loads both big . . .

He moves the dirt
from place to place,
Then dumps it with
a happy face.

. . . and small,

One final load spills on
the heap (*crrrunch!*);
Now Dump Truck's tired
and wants to sleep.

He lowers his bed, locks his gate,
Rests his wheels; it's getting late.
He dims his lights, then shuts his doors,
And soon his engine slows to snores.

Shh . . . goodnight, Dump Truck, goodnight.

Pushing with his mighty blade,
Bulldozer works to smooth the grade.
He clears the way to level ground,
And fills the air with thunderous sound
(*rooaaar!*).

No one's as tough
and strong as he,
But now he's sleepy

as

can

be.

He puffs some smoke

out of his stack,

Turns off his engine,

stops his track.

He curls into his soft dirt bed
And dreams of busy days ahead.

Shh . . . goodnight, Bulldozer, goodnight.

Scooping gravel, dirt, and sand,
Excavator shapes the land.
He digs and lifts throughout the day (*arrgh!*),
But now it's time to end his play.

A few more holes to dig and soon
He'll roll to bed beneath the moon.

He twirls upon his bumpy track,
Pulls up his boom, stretches his back.
He sets his scoop down on the ground
And snuggles up without a sound.

Shh . . . goodnight, Excavator, goodnight.

These big, big trucks, so tough and loud,
They work so hard, so rough, and proud.
Tomorrow is another day,
Another chance to work and play.

Turn off your engines, stop your tracks,
Relax your wheels, your stacks, and backs.
No more huffing and puffing, team:
It's time to rest your heads and dream.

Construction site, all tucked in tight,
The day is done, turn off the light.

Great work today! Now . . . shh . . . goodnight.

For one blue-eyed boy and one brown-eyed boy and
the world of wonder and possibility I see through their
eyes. And, always, for Faith. —S. R.

To Jan, for sharing a dream. —T. L.

ISBN 978-0-545-48788-7

12 11 10 9 8 7 6 5 4 3 2 1   12 13 14 15 16 17/0

Printed in the U.S.A.   08

This edition first printing, September 2012

Book design by Tom Lichtenheld and Amelia May Anderson
Typeset in Mr. Eaves Bold
The illustrations in this book were rendered in Neocolor wax oil
pastels on Mi-Teintes paper.